Dora's Easter Basket

adapted by Sarah Willson
from the screenplay by Eric Weiner
illustrated by Susan Hall

Simon Spotlight/Nick Jr.
New York   London   Toronto   Sydney   Singapore

Based on the TV series *Dora the Explorer*® as seen on Nick Jr.®

SIMON SPOTLIGHT
An imprint of Simon & Schuster Children's Publishing Division
1230 Avenue of the Americas, New York, New York 10020
Copyright © 2003 Viacom International Inc.
SIMON SPOTLIGHT and colophon are registered trademarks of Simon & Schuster.
Manufactured in the United States of America

10 12 14 16 15 13 11
ISBN 0-689-85240-1

Say it in Spanish!

Hola:	OH-la	Cinco:	SING-koh
Vámonos:	VA-mo-nos	Seis:	SAYs
Buenos Días:	BWEH-nos DEE-ahs	Siete:	See-EH-tay
Muy Bien:	MWEE Bee-YEN	Ocho:	OH-cho
Uno:	OO-no	Nueve:	New-EH-vay
Dos:	DOHs	Diez:	Dee-EHZ
Tres:	TREHs	Once:	ON-say
Cuatro:	KWAH-troh	Doce:	DOH-say

¡*Hola!* I'm Dora. Boots and I are going on an egg hunt. *Mami* and *Papi* hid twelve special eggs for us to find.

Each egg has a prize inside. The big, yellow egg has the largest prize of all. Will you help us find all twelve eggs?

Where should we look for the eggs? Let's ask the Map! Say, "Map!" The Map says we should look for eggs by the Duck Pond and at the Farm. Then we should search for the big, yellow egg at Grandma's House. Come on! *¡Vámonos!*

Do you see any eggs? Where?

How many eggs do we have?

We have to watch out for Swiper the fox. He'll try to swipe our eggs. If you see him, say, "Swiper, no swiping!"

We stopped Swiper! Thanks for helping. Let's see what prizes are inside our eggs.

Can you tell which prizes came from which eggs?
Map told us to look near the Duck Pond. Do you see the pond?

We made it to the Duck Pond. Look! There's a *Mami* duck and her ducklings. How many eggs do you see?

Uh-oh. How are we going to get the eggs off those lily pads?

Let's check Backpack. Backpack always has everything we need.

Can you find something in Backpack that will help us scoop up those eggs?

The net worked! Good job! Wow, look at the prizes that were inside the eggs. Can you tell which prize came from which egg?

Do you see another egg? Oh, it's on the sleepy sloth's tummy! We have to wake her up and ask for the egg. Can you help us? We need to use Spanish to wake her up. Can you say, *"Buenos días"*?

You did it! She gave us the egg. See the prize that was inside? You wind it up to make it go. Uh-oh, it's rolling away. Follow that car!

Can you find the path
that leads to the Farm?

Here's our friend Tico the squirrel. *¡Hola,* Tico! Tico says we'll find one egg next to an animal that says, "oink," and one egg next to an animal that says, "moo."

Great job! Tico says there is one more egg to find at the Farm. Do you see it? Show Tico the way to the egg.

He got there! Great! *¡Muy bien!*

Let's see the prizes inside. Can you tell which prizes came out of which eggs?

Now let's go to Grandma's House!

We made it to Grandma's House. But we still haven't found the big, yellow egg. Do you see it?

Yeah, there it is!
There's another big egg. But it doesn't look like the others. Who could be inside that egg?

It's Swiper! He'll try to swipe the egg. Say, "Swiper, no swiping!"

Did we find all the eggs? Let's count them in Spanish and see:
uno, dos, tres, cuatro, cinco, seis, siete,
ocho, nueve, diez, once, doce.
Twelve—we did it!

Now we can open the big, yellow egg. It's got the biggest prize of all. Can you guess what's inside?

Hooray! We did it! Look at all the treats that were inside the big, yellow egg!